For my family, and yours.

WHEN WE SAY BLACK LIVES MATTER

written and illustrated by

MAXINE BENEBA CLARKE

CANDLEWICK PRESS

Little one,

when we say
Black Lives Matter,

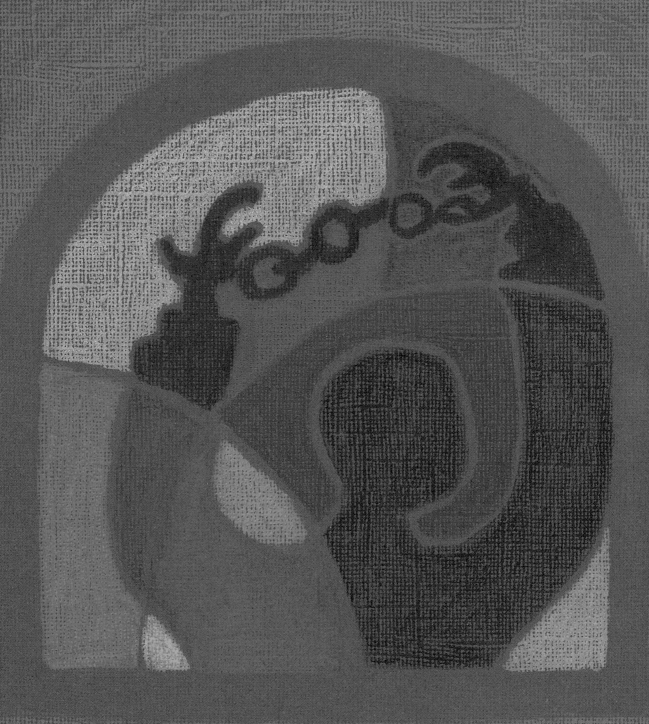

That we deserve to be
treated with basic RESPECT,
and that history's done us wrong.

Little love, when we call out
Black Lives Matter,
we're saying *walk with us,*
raise your voice:

When we scream out Black Lives Matter,
and we march, against falling night,
we're saying enough is **enough** is **enough**
and we need to put things right.

Darling, when we sing that Black Lives Matter, and we're dancing through the streets, we're saying: fear will not destroy our joy, defiance in our feet.

When we *whisper*
Black Lives Matter,
we're remembering
the past.

All the terrible things
that were said and done,

we're saying they
trouble our hearts.

When
we
sob
that
Black Lives Matter,

we're saying trouble
still STALKS,
to this day,

that we've seen it
monster in the shadows

and must all help **drive** it away.

My sweet, when we **bellow**
Black Lives Matter, we're saying:
ain't no freedom till we get ours.

And *all* Black folk still suffering,
we'll **STAND** with you, we vow.

When we **smile**
Black Lives Matter,
we're raising our spirits high.

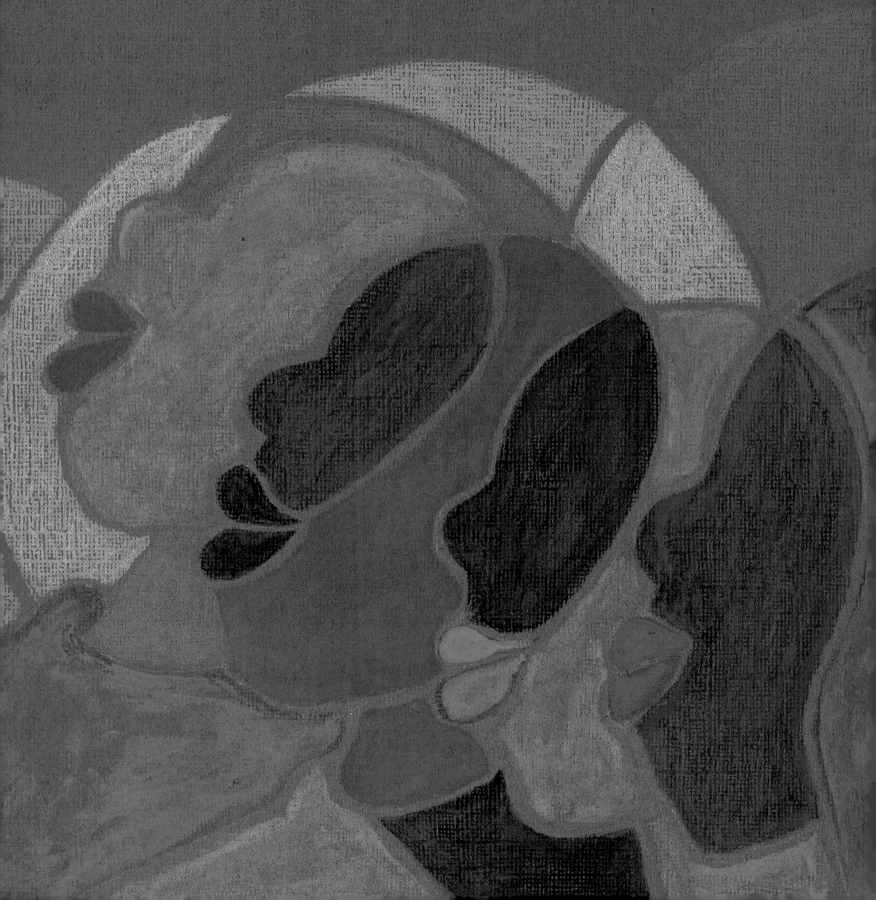

We're saying
we are here,

and we are **enough**.

Black-beautiful-brave,
my child.

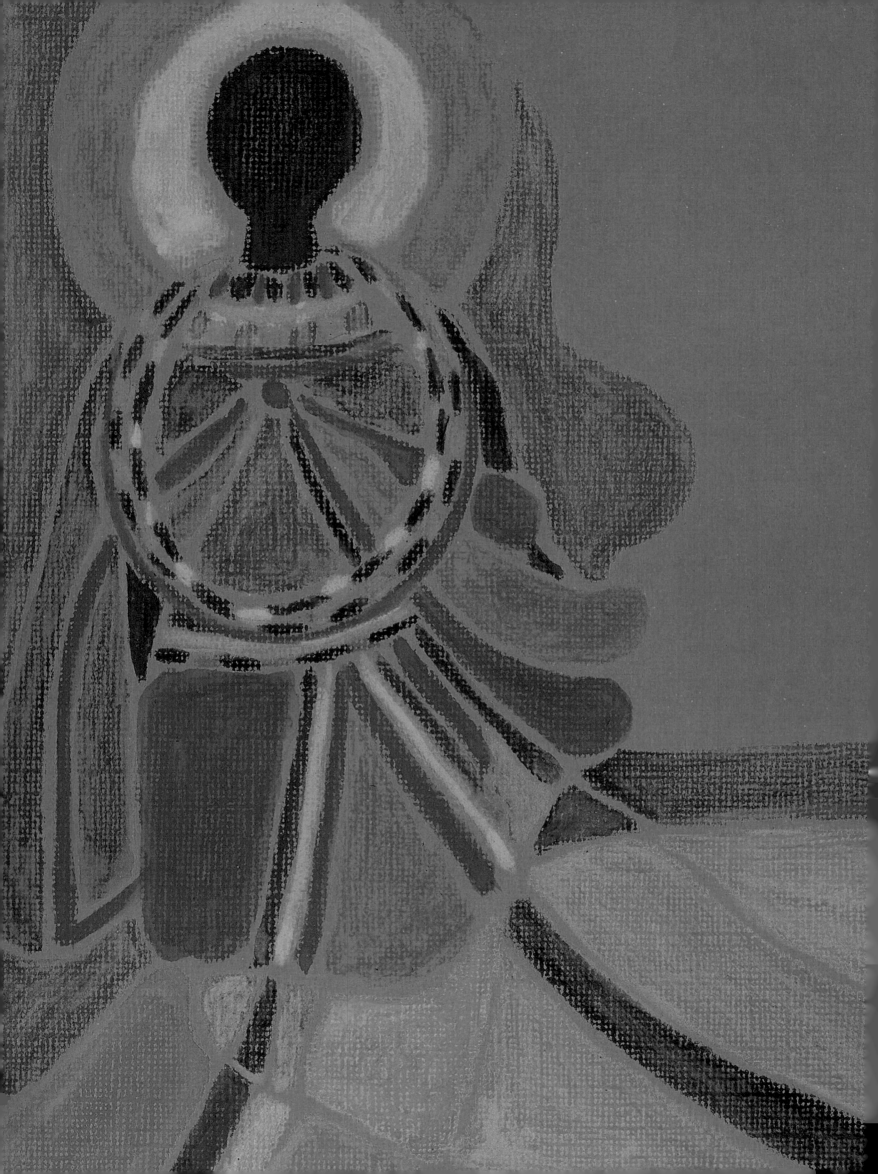

When we **laugh** that Black Lives Matter, that's the ancestors, inside:

a-thundering on djembe drums
and guiding us, steady, to rise.

When we *know* that
Black Lives Matter,
then darling, we know our worth:
that we are as precious
as every soul
whose story has
journeyed the earth.

We see you, Black-child-magic,
your RADIANT Black shine.

First US edition 2021
First published by Hachette Australia 2020

Library of Congress Catalog Card Number pending
ISBN 978-1-5362-2238-8

21 22 23 24 25 26 APS 10 9 8 7 6 5 4 3 2 1

Printed in Humen, Dongguan, China

This book was typeset in Flat Brush.
The illustrations were done in watercolor pencil and collage.

Candlewick Press
99 Dover Street
Somerville, Massachusetts 02144

www.candlewick.com